BARNEY'S SAND CASTLE

by Stephanie Calmenson
illustrated by Sheila Beckett

A Golden Book • New York
Western Publishing Company, Inc., Racine, Wisconsin 53404

BARNEY needed one more thing
to put on his sand castle.

"Mama!" he said.
"May I go for a walk?

I want to find something special
for the top of my sand castle."

"Of course," said his mama. "But you
may go only as far as the lifeguard stand."

Barney started off.
He took his pail. Near the
water's edge he found
a starfish.

It moved when Barney touched
it with a stick.

Now Barney knew
the starfish was alive.

He left it on the sand and
went on down the beach.

Barney saw all kinds of pretty seashells.

He put some of the prettiest
in his pail.

Barney saw birds looking
for food in the water.

One bird swooped down and came
back up with a fish in its beak!

Barney found two smooth white pieces of driftwood. He put them in his pail.

A prickly sea urchin lay in a
tide pool. Barney left it there.

Three crabs were crawling up the beach.
One waved its longest claw back and forth.

Barney walked carefully
around them.

The lifeguard stand was very close now,
so Barney knew he could not go much
farther. He saw a bug lying on its back.

"Hello, bug," said Barney.
"I will help you."

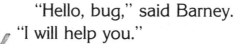

He gently turned the bug over. "Ladybug, ladybug, fly away home," he said.

Barney wondered if he
would ever find the right
thing for his sand castle.

Then he saw something
sticking up out of the sand.

It was a long, beautiful bird feather. "This is just right!" said Barney happily.

He ran all the way back to the castle.

He took the shells and the wood out of his
pail and used them to decorate his castle.

Then he put the feather on the very top.

"Mama! Mama!" he shouted.
"My castle is finished!"

"It's beautiful!" said Mama. "I will take a picture of you with your castle."

And she did.